Sheila Lavelle

Sheila Lavelle was born in Gateshead, County Durham, in 1939. She says she spent her childhood reading anything she could lay her hands on, and by the age of ten she had decided she would be a writer.

Her first book was published in 1977, after she had married, raised two sons, and been an infant school teacher for ten years.

Sheila now lives in a seaside cottage in Galloway, Scotland, with her husband Derek and two border collies called Ben and Lucy. She likes to spend her mornings writing, and her afternoons walking the dogs.

As well as writing, Sheila is interested in gardening, bird-watching, spinning, weaving, listening to Italian operas, reading, cooking and dog obedience training. She has recently become a grandmother.

British Library Cataloguing in Publication Data
Lavelle, Shiela
Fish stew.
I. Title II. Church, Caroline III. Series
823'.914 [F]
ISBN 1 85543 018 5

First edition

Published by Ladybird Books Ltd Loughborough Leicestershire UK

Ladybird Books Inc Auburn Maine 04210 USA

Paperbird is an imprint of Ladybird Books Ltd

Twist in the Tale books are designed,
conceived and originated by Signpost Books Ltd

Printed in England (3)

A Twist in the Tale Book

Fish Stew

by

SHEILA LAVELLE

illustrated by

CAROLINE CHURCH

Paperbird

PAPERBIRD

CHAPTER 1

Annie didn't know the dog was following her until Mr Grump yelled at her in the Burger Bar.

'Get that scruffy thing out of here!' he shouted. 'Can't you read?' He pointed a fat greasy finger at a notice.

Annie went red and stared at him. What scruffy thing? What could the stupid man be talking about? Then she felt a damp nose touch her hand and she looked down into the saddest pair of brown eyes she had ever seen. A small hairy brown dog, with a filthy matted coat and with his ribs sticking out through his sides, was gazing up at her and sniffing at the bag of food she had just picked up off the counter.

He looked as if he hadn't eaten for weeks, and for soft-hearted Annie there was only one thing to do. She took the dog outside, and right there on the pavement she delved into the bag, unwrapped the cheeseburger which was to have been her own Saturday lunch, and gave it to the starving animal.

The cheeseburger disappeared in seconds. The dog polished the ground with his tongue, then wagged his tail eagerly, his eyes fixed on the bag. But Annie remembered the rest of her family waiting for their lunch, and she didn't dare give him any more.

'Go home, dog,' she urged, although by the look of him he didn't have one. 'Go on. Home!' The dog wagged his tail harder and jumped up to lick Annie's face. She hugged him to her, wondering what to do.

Annie had wanted a dog since she was five years old, when the family had spent a holiday on a farm and she had fallen in love with a black and white sheepdog called Ben. Her mum and dad had said no, their small house was full already, and there just wasn't room for a dog. Annie had nagged for weeks, but had finally given up the idea. Until now.

The dog sat at her feet and gazed at her hopefully, his head on one side. This was a very small dog, Annie thought. Surely they could find room for him. She made up her mind it was worth a try.

'Come on then, skinny,' she said, and set off for home, the dog bounding joyfully by her side. Turning the corner past the church, she slowed her steps nervously as she saw Max the Magnificent and his gang coming along the street.

He called himself Max the Magnificent, but he was only a horrible pimply little weed who bullied all the younger children in Annie's class at school, and roamed the streets at weekends looking for trouble. Annie hated him almost as much as she

hated the lumpy mashed potatoes and watery cabbage that were served up at school dinners.

'Cor, look at that!' one of the gang was saying. 'Annie Watson's gone and got herself a dog.'

'Call that a dog?' sneered Max scornfully. 'It's more like a walking bag of bones!' And the whole gang fell about laughing as if it were the wittiest thing they had ever heard.

Annie stood still, her heart thudding against her T-shirt. This gang was well known for snatching other kids' belongings, and she clutched the bag of hamburgers closely to her chest. She needn't have worried, however, for as the gang drew nearer, their eyes fixed greedily on the tell-tale Macdougals's paper sack, a low growl started up in the dog's throat. The growl grew into a snarl, and, to Annie's relief, Max the Magnificent and all his cowardly gang hurriedly moved back to allow her and the dog to go past.

'Thanks, Tiger!' Annie said gleefully as they ran off together towards home, and he wagged his skinny tail harder than ever.

Annie let herself into the hall with her key. She quickly pushed the dog through the door of the front room, which was never used by the family except when visitors came to tea, and where he would be safe for a while.

'Stay here, Tiger,' she whispered. 'And don't make a sound.' She watched the dog sniff suspiciously round the furniture before curling up under the sofa in a dark corner. The curtains were half-closed, and most of the light came from Annie's dad's beloved fish tank, with its fancy shells and lumps of rock and rustic arches, all lit up with coloured lights.

Annie's gran said it wasn't natural for a

grown man to spend so much of his time gawping at a load of fish, and Annie secretly agreed, although she never said so. She wouldn't hurt her father for the world. He worked hard all week driving a truck, and if his way of relaxing on Saturday nights was to watch tropical fish swimming around in a tank, it was up to him, Annie thought.

She heard Gran's voice from the living room, bawling above the noise from the telly.

'Is that you, Annie? Where have you been? We're all starving.' Gran hobbled into the hall on her stick, her eyes blinking short-sightedly behind her glasses.

'I'm here, Gran,' said Annie, shutting the front room door. 'Here are the hamburgers.' She held up the bag.

'About time too,' grumbled Gran, going back to the living room, where she could be heard yelling at Annie's brothers, Tim and Pete, to stop fighting and to get cleaned up for lunch. Annie carried the paper sack through the living room to the kitchen.

Lunch was a rowdy affair as usual. Annie's mum, in paint-spattered jeans and smock, joined the family only briefly from her attic studio where she was working on a large oil-painting for an exhibition. She only smiled dreamily at

the boys' noisy pranks, and Annie knew it wasn't a good time to mention the dog. She would wait until Dad came home that evening, she decided.

Annie's stomach rumbled as she watched the family tuck into their food. After saying that she'd eaten her cheeseburger on the way home she had to make do with bread and butter, but luckily Gran had baked one of her delicious apple pies, which helped to fill up some space. Annie's thoughts kept returning to the dog, and she escaped as soon as she could and went to look for him.

It took her eyes a few moments to adjust to the poor light in the front room. 'Where are you, Tiger?' she said softly. He wasn't under the sofa where she had left him. Then a small crunching sound made her look towards the corner where the fish tank stood on its shelf. And what she saw made Annie's legs go as limp as old lettuce.

The dog was standing on his hind legs on the stool in front of the tank. His head was in the water, and he was munching hungrily away at the contents.

'Tiger!' said Annie sharply. 'Get out of there!' The dog wagged his tail and looked at her, water dripping from his jaws onto the carpet. Bits of green weed dangled from his chin, making him look like some strange kind of billy-goat.

Annie went closer and gazed fearfully into the tank. Then her eyes widened and she clutched the dog in horror, for there wasn't a single fish to be seen. The harlequins, the swordtails, the guppies, and even the beautiful striped angelfish, every one had vanished.

'Flippin' heck!' gasped Annie. 'Flippin' bloomin' heck!' And she sat down on the floor with a thump.

CHAPTER 2

Annie and Tiger dashed down the road and just managed to catch the two o'clock bus to Burnbridge. The dog curled up on the floor under the seat and began to snore at once. Sleeping off the effects of his fish dinner, Annie thought with a shudder.

She took her purse from her pocket to count her money, but the result was depressing. After emptying her piggy-bank with a kitchen knife, bullying her brothers into lending their Saturday pocket-money, and borrowing a pound from a grumbling, reluctant Gran, Annie had managed to raise only six pounds and a few pence. Whether this would be enough to re-stock a tankful of tropical fish she had no idea. No doubt she'd find out when she reached the pet shop in Burnbridge, she told herself gloomily.

'Burnbridge?' said a voice in Annie's ear. 'That'll be fifty pence and half price for the dog.' The bus conductor, a red-faced man with a purple nose and hair like a lavatory brush, held out his hand.

Annie groaned. She'd forgotten that the bus fares had gone up. After allowing for the fare home she wouldn't have much left to buy fish.

'Do I have to pay for the dog?' she pleaded. 'He's a very small dog, and he isn't occupying a seat.'

The conductor shook his head. 'Makes no difference, sunshine,' he said. 'Them's the rules. I'd lose my job if an inspector got on. Seventy-five pence, please.'

Annie handed over the money with a sigh. Keeping a dog was turning out to be an expensive business, she thought ruefully. She glanced down at the dog's skinny body, twitching in sleep as if he were chasing salmon in his dreams, and she told herself fiercely it didn't matter

how much he cost her. He was hers now, whatever happened, and whatever the rest of the family had to say.

It would be Dad who had the final word. That was why Annie knew it was important to replace the fish before he came home tonight. And in spite of the trouble she was in, Annie couldn't help giggling out loud as she imagined the conversation. 'By the way, Dad, I brought this dog home, and he was so hungry he ate all your fish. You don't mind if I keep him, do you?' Normally a quiet, placid man, Annie's dad could really blow his top when something upset him, and truck-drivers know a lot of rude words.

Annie scrambled off the bus in Burnbridge with Tiger at her heels and headed straight towards the High Street, where the pet shop was. She had only gone a few yards when she found her way blocked by a tall figure in uniform.

'Now then, young lady,' said a loud voice. 'Is that your dog?'

Annie looked up at the policeman's stern face and felt her cheeks turn red. What could she say? If she said the dog was a stray the policeman might take him from her. And when you've wanted a dog as long as Annie had, it wasn't easy to give up your very first chance of owning one.

'Er . . . yes,' she managed to stammer. 'He is mine. His name's Tiger.'

The policeman smiled at her and his moustache wriggled like a large furry caterpillar.

'Well, I'm afraid he must wear his collar and lead in town,' he said. 'It's the law, you know. To stop him being a danger to traffic.' He bent down and patted Tiger on the head, and Tiger licked the policeman's hand. 'He looks as if a bath and a good meal wouldn't do him any harm, either,' the policeman added, giving Annie a hard look.

'Annie gulped. 'He hasn't got a collar and lead yet,' she confessed. 'I only got him this morning.' Then Annie noticed that they were standing right outside a hardware store, and she had a sudden brainwave. 'I was just about to buy him one,' she fibbed quickly. 'In there.' She pointed at the doorway of the shop.

'Right, then,' said the policeman. 'Off you go. I'll stay here and hang on to him until you come back.'

The policeman slipped a string round the dog's neck and grinned at Annie encouragingly. Annie dithered for a moment on the pavement. This wasn't what she had expected at all, but in the end she had no choice. She left Tiger sitting dolefully beside the policeman's large boots and hurried into the shop. And, to her disgust, the cheapest collar and lead she could find cost her a precious two pounds seventy-five pence out of her rapidly dwindling fish fund.

The policeman watched approvingly as

Annie fastened the collar and lead onto the ecstatic Tiger, who bounced up and down in delight at her return. Then, breathing a sigh of relief as the policeman finally walked off down the street, Annie hurried away towards the pet shop, doing complicated sums in her head and trying to guess the price of angelfish.

She needn't have bothered, for when she reached the middle of the High Street, where the pet shop had been a week or two before, all Annie found was a wasteland. The pet shop had been totally demolished. Dust and debris blew around the gutter and into Annie's eyes as she stared disbelievingly at the piles of bricks and rubble which had once been a fascinating wonderland full of puppies and kittens and hamsters and rabbits and a crested cockatoo called Wally.

A man in a dusty blue overall shovelling rubbish into a wheelbarrow saw Annie standing there as pale as paper.

'Looking for the pet shop?' he said, and Annie managed a nod. 'Closed for re-building,' the man told her cheerfully. 'Re-opening in three months' time, better than ever.'

'Three months!' Annie's voice was faint and her mouth felt as dry as the Sahara. She couldn't wait three months. She needed those fish tonight, or there was no hope whatsoever of her dad letting her keep the dog. Now what was she going to do?

CHAPTER 3

Annie was still standing forlornly in the street when she heard somebody shouting her name. She looked up and saw a plump, curly haired figure crossing the road towards her. It was her best friend, Tanya, and Annie waved thankfully, full of hope once more. Tanya was the brightest girl in her class at school, and if she couldn't think of a way out of this dreadful mess then nobody could.

'Hi, Annie,' said Tanya. 'Got yourself a dog at last, have you?' She bent down and ruffled Tiger's ears. 'Flippin' heck!' she said. 'What a scruffy little mongrel! I hope it hasn't got fleas.'

Annie shook her head dolefully. 'I wouldn't be surprised,' she said. 'And he's already got me into the worst stew I've ever been in my whole life.'

Tanya's black eyes danced. 'What?' she said. 'Worse than the time you pushed Amelia Featherstone-Forbes into the swimming pool? That caused a good old row, I remember.' And Tanya giggled at the thought.

'Much worse than that,' said Annie earnestly. 'Promise you won't laugh if I tell you?'

Tanya promised. Then she tucked her arm into Annie's and the two friends walked down a side street and into a little park. There they sat on a quiet bench while Annie poured out the whole sad tale. And in spite of her promise, Tanya giggled so much she almost fell off the bench.

'Sorry, Annie,' she gasped, stuffing her hanky into her mouth to stifle her laughter. 'You mean he actually ate all your father's pet fish? It's the funniest thing I've ever heard!'

Annie got up and stomped off in disgust. 'Come on, Tiger,' she said to the

dog. 'I should have known better than to expect any help from her! We'll manage on our own from now on.'

Tanya put on a serious face. 'Come back, Sulkypants,' she said. 'I won't laugh any more, I promise. I think I've got an idea. Now, listen. The pet shop at Salterton is miles away and they'd be closed by the time we got there, so that's no good. But did you know there's a fair on at Clayton's Meadow, just on the edge of town?'

'Fair?' said Annie. 'Who wants to go to a fair? I've hardly got any money left as it is.'

Tanya spoke slowly and distinctly as if she were talking to a three-year-old. 'What do they give away as prizes at fairs, Annie Watson?' she said patiently.

'Coconuts,' said Annie, which set Tanya giggling all over again.

'No, not coconuts, stupid,' she spluttered. 'Goldfish! They give away goldfish! In little plastic bags!'

Annie stared at Tanya. 'I don't want goldfish,' she said. 'I want guppies and swordtails and harlequins and angelfish.'

'Listen,' Tanya urged, grabbing Annie's arm. 'Goldfish are fish, aren't they? So long as there's something swimming around in that tank your dad might not notice the difference for a couple of days. Then we'll have time to get to Salterton on Monday. I can get some money out of my savings account, and you know Salterton's got the biggest pet shop in the world!'

Annie kicked at the grass and stared at the ground for a long time. Deep down she knew it wouldn't work. The first thing her dad always did the minute he got home was to go and look at his beloved fish. But goldfish would be better than nothing, she supposed. And maybe she could think of a way to distract her dad for once. Maybe it was worth a try.

She looked at Tanya's eager face and gave a weak grin. 'OK. What are we waiting for?' she said. 'Come on, Tiger. We're going to the fair.'

They heard the fairground music long before they reached Clayton's Meadow and quickened their steps at the sound of it. And it turned out to be just the sort of fair that Annie loved, with old-fashioned roundabouts and swings, coconut shies and rifle ranges, and dozens of stalls selling everything from hot dogs to gobstoppers.

'Look,' said Tanya, suddenly poking Annie's ribs. 'There's somebody with a goldfish. Let's ask him where he got it.' She ran off to speak to a red-haired teenager with a goldfish swimming about in a plastic bag, while Annie dragged Tiger firmly away from the hot dog stall.

'Come on, Annie,' called Tanya. 'It's over here. And it looks as easy as pie!'

It didn't look as easy as pie to Annie. To win a goldfish you paid twenty pence for

three rubber rings. You had to throw the rings onto numbered hooks on a board, and a score of fifty or over got you a prize.

'It's not possible,' she grumbled into Tanya's ear. 'It's a waste of money, if you ask me.'

'Don't be so wet, Annie,' said Tanya. 'Of course it's possible. We've seen people walking out with goldfish, haven't we? Come on, give me twenty pence. I've only got my bus fare.'

An hour later Tanya, red-faced and worried, had found out that winning a

goldfish wasn't as easy as it looked. She mopped her brow with her hanky and handed over their last twenty pence to the grinning attendant.

'This is it, Annie,' she breathed. 'It's now or never.' And she threw the first of her three rings.

Annie shut her eyes and didn't dare look. She had tried to make Tanya stop after her first fruitless ten minutes, but for Tanya, who was mad about all sports and hated to be a loser at anything, this had turned out to be some sort of challenge.

'Twenty-five,' called the astonished attendant, and Annie opened her eyes. Sure enough, the ring had landed on the hook at the top of the board, a score of twenty-five points. Tanya winked at her and threw the second hoop straight after the first. It hit the hook and bounced onto the floor. Tanya heaved a sigh of despair.

'Last ring,' she said resignedly. She stared hard at the board for a moment, muttering something under her breath. Then she took careful aim and sent the ring soaring towards the hook.

'Twenty-five again!' shouted the attendant, his eyebrows disappearing into his bushy orange hair. 'Fifty scored. One

goldfish coming up. Thank you, Miss. Come along now, everybody. See how easy it is! Twenty pence for three rings!'

Tiger barked and jumped about in delight as Tanya did three cartwheels one after the other on the grass, whooping with glee.

'I knew I could do it!' she panted. 'I just knew it.'

Annie looked at the lonely little goldfish swimming in its bag of water and felt sorry for it. But not nearly as sorry as she felt for herself. All they'd managed to get after all that time was one measly little goldfish. They must be crazy or something.

Tanya looked at Annie's face. 'What's up, Grumpy-knickers?' she said. 'We won a goldfish, didn't we?'

'One stupid goldfish won't fool my dad,' Annie said miserably, blinking back tears. 'And apart from that, we've spent all the money we had. Including our bus fare. How the heck are we going to get home?'

CHAPTER 4

Two hours later Annie was trudging along the last stretch of riverbank between Burnbridge and the village where she and Tanya lived. Tired and hungry, her feet sore and blistered, she was fed up and miserable. With no money left, and no way of getting any, there had been no choice but to walk home. And even Tiger, who had set off in such great spirits, his tail wagging non-stop, now limped along dejectedly and kept giving Annie reproachful looks. I don't mind a walk, he seemed to be saying, but nobody mentioned a marathon.

Annie stopped to wait for Tanya, who was trailing along behind, carrying the goldfish in its plastic bag. 'Come on,

Tanya. It's nearly six o'clock,' she said. 'My dad will be back at seven, and I want to put the goldfish in the tank before he gets home.'

Tanya hurried to catch up, a worried expression on her face. 'I don't think it looks very well, Annie,' she said unhappily. And she held up the bag for Annie to see.

The goldfish, confined in its tiny space, did not look well at all. It lay on its side in the water, hardly moving its fins, and rapidly opening and closing its mouth as if gasping for air.

'It can't breathe,' said Annie, who had

learnt a bit about fish from her father. 'Look, the poor thing's got no oxygen left.'

Tanya stared. 'Fish don't breathe, stupid,' she said. 'They live on the oxygen in the water.'

'Not when they've used it all up, they don't,' said Annie. 'We'll have to give it fresh water, or it'll die.' She took the bag from Tanya and unfastened the tie at the top. Kneeling down on the bank, and holding the bag carefully so that the fish didn't escape, she tipped out some of the stale water and allowed fresh water to flow in.

'There, that's better,' she said. But her voice was suddenly drowned by Tiger's furious barking. Then everything started to happen so fast that Annie didn't have time to think. Tanya shrieked a warning but it was too late. Heavy feet thundered along the towpath, wild war-whoops rang through the air, and Max the Magnificent and his gang came charging towards her along the bank.

Before Annie could get to her feet two rough hands shoved her from behind and she fell into the river with a splash. The water was not very deep at that point, and Annie was in no danger, but she was soaked to the skin and covered in mud. And when she groped around to retrieve the plastic bag, she was just in time to see

the goldfish dart out of the opening and swim away into deep water as if its life depended on it.

Howls of fright made her turn round, and in spite of the mud plastered to her clothes and the wet hair dripping into her eyes, Annie danced with glee as she saw Max the Magnificent, a large hole in the seat of his jeans, fleeing into the distance after his band of warriors. And there was Tiger, trotting proudly back to her along the towpath, his tail held high, and a piece of torn blue material held firmly in his jaws.

'Are you OK?' said Tanya anxiously, helping Annie out of the water. 'Oh, lord, Annie! Don't say you've lost the goldfish!'

Annie could only shiver and shake and laugh and nod her head speechlessly. The goldfish was much better off where it was.

CHAPTER 5

It was twenty minutes to seven by the hall clock when Annie sneaked in through the front door of the house and squelched upstairs to her bedroom. Luckily Gran and the boys were in the living room watching television, so she shoved Tiger under the bed while she had a quick shower and scrambled into dry clothes.

'Stay there, Tiger,' she told him firmly, then she shut the bedroom door and ran upstairs to the attic studio where her mother was still at work.

'Mum,' she said, sticking her head round the door. 'Could you do me a favour?'

Annie's mum wiped her paintbrush on a rag and stepped back to admire her work. Annie went and stood beside her to have to look. It was a painting of a loaf of bread, a bottle of wine and a bunch of grapes, and it had taken Annie's mum so long to paint that the grapes on the table in front of the easel had gone rotten and the bread had turned mouldly. But the picture was lovely, and Annie said so.

'It's great, Mum,' she said, hoping to put her mother in a good mood.

Annie's mum gazed at the picture. 'It's not bad, is it?' she said thoughtfully. 'I'll be glad when it's finished, though, so that I can paint something else. I'm sick of bread and grapes.'

Annie took a deep breath. This was her chance. 'Can you paint fish, Mum?' she said, in a casual voice as if it didn't matter in the least.

Annie's mum turned her dreamy blue eyes to her daughter. 'Fish? What sort of fish?' she said curiously. And Annie blurted out what it was she wanted.

Five minutes later Annie scurried helter-skelter down the stairs to the front room, a roll of sticky tape and a water-

colour sketch in her hand. The sketch was a picture of tropical fish swimming in a tank, with shells and weed and gravel and coloured rustic arches. It was probably a stupid idea, but it was the only thing Annie could think of, and it was now five minutes to seven.

Annie opened the door of the front room and hurried to the corner where the fish tank stood on its shelf. Working quickly and silently, she taped the sketch to the glass on the outside of the tank and stood back to see the effect. And it wasn't bad at all if you didn't look too closely. The lights over the tank shone through the paper and lit the brightly-coloured fish, and you could almost believe they were alive. Annie was wondering ruefully

just how long it would fool her dad when the door opened behind her.

'Dad!' gasped Annie, turning round with a guilty start. 'You're home early!'

Annie's dad, tall, dark, and with shoulders like an American football player, grinned at her from the doorway. In his hand was a small plastic bucket with air-holes in the lid.

'It's after seven, sweetheart,' he said, coming into the room, 'What have you been doing with the fish tank?' He peered at it in surprise.

Annie grabbed his hand. 'Dad!' she said frantically. 'Don't bother with the fish tonight! Let's go for a walk! Let's go to the park or something! Anything! Please, Dad!' She dragged him towards the door.

'Hang on, Annie,' he laughed. 'What's the hurry? There's something I want to do first, then I'll go anywhere you like.' Annie's heart turned over as he went back to the tank and sat down on the stool in front of it. This was it. Now she was for it, Annie thought.

She waited dumbly for the howls of rage but none came. Her dad merely stared at the painting stuck to the glass and scratched his head, baffled. Then he looked at Annie for an explanation. 'Did you do this?' he said.

And that was when Annie decided that the only thing left was to tell the truth. She hurled herself at his chest and flung her arms round his neck and sobbed out the whole story about the dog and the hamburgers and the dog eating all the fish and the pet shop being demolished and going to the fairground and winning the goldfish and the boys pushing her in the river and the goldfish swimming away and how Mum had painted the sketch and . . . and . . . and . . .

Several times Annie's dad tried to

interrupt her, but she wouldn't stop until she had confessed everything, and finally he let her go on until her voice tailed away into a hiccup. Then he dried her face on his big white hanky and looked into her eyes.

'I've got something to show you, Annie,' he said, and to Annie's astonishment she saw that he wasn't cross in the least. In fact, he was doing his best not to laugh. He picked up the plastic bucket from the floor and took off the lid. 'Look at these little beauties!' he said.

Annie sniffed and hiccupped and sniffed again. Then she stared into the bucket. About a dozen little creatures were swimming around in the water or clambering out onto some bits of rock. They were round and black, with shells like turtles, and little black heads and feet.

'Turtles?' said Annie wonderingly.

'Terrapins!' said Annie's dad proudly, tipping them out of the bucket into the fish tank. 'Much more interesting than those boring old fish. Listen, Annie. I took the fish to work on Monday, and my mate Ted swopped them for these. Cute, aren't they?'

Annie stared at her dad, her mouth open. 'So there weren't any fish . . .?' She stopped speechless.

'The fish haven't been there all week,' said Annie's dad, smiling. 'That dog of yours only ate some weed. Or maybe he was just thirsty, I don't know. But he certainly didn't eat any of my fish. There weren't any there to eat!'

Annie felt weak with relief. She closed her eyes and rested her head for a moment against her dad's chest. Then she thought of something.

'So can we keep the dog?' she said, her voice coming out in a sort of squeak.

'Let's go and have a look at him,' grinned Annie's dad, taking her hand. 'I bet you anything you like he's hungry!'

If you've enjoyed reading this Twist in the Tale book look out for others in the Paperbird series.

You're NOT *My Parents*

by R. L. Stine

Things started to go really wrong one Saturday morning. First of all Snappy the dog had disappeared, and why were Rob's parents behaving in such a strange way. He was sure they had been taken over by aliens. They were *not* his parents! But who would believe him?

Whizzkid

by Tessa Krailing

Bingo Barnes was sure that he would build a real time machine one day. The old bath in the shed didn't quite go anywhere, but all it needed was little more work and then he would show them. And he did.

Nine Lives

by Carolyn Sloan

Wellington Smith thought there was something rather strange about Jane Grant's cat Zodiac. When he went to help her with her new word processor, he began to find out what it was. But the old lady swore him to secrecy.